Tucholsky Wagner Zola Scott Sydow Freud Schlegel
Turgenev Wallace Fonatne Twain Walther von der Vogelweide Fouqué Friedrich II. von Preußen
Weber Freiligrath Frey Kant Ernst
Fechner Fichte Weiße Rose von Fallersleben Richthofen Frommel
Engels Fielding Hölderlin
Fehrs Faber Flaubert Eichendorff Tacitus Dumas
Eliasberg Ebner Eschenbach
Feuerbach Maximilian I. von Habsburg Fock Zweig
Ewald Eliot Vergil
Goethe Elisabeth von Österreich London
Mendelssohn Balzac Shakespeare Dostojewski Ganghofer
Trackl Lichtenberg Rathenau Doyle Gjellerup
Stevenson Hambruch
Mommsen Tolstoi Lenz Droste-Hülshoff
Thoma Hanrieder
Dach von Arnim Hägele Hauff Humboldt
Verne Hagen Hauptmann
Reuter Rousseau Gautier
Karrillon Garschin Baudelaire
Defoe Hebbel
Damaschke Descartes Hegel Kussmaul Herder
Wolfram von Eschenbach Schopenhauer Rilke George
Darwin Dickens Grimm Jerome
Bronner Melville Bebel Proust
Campe Horváth Aristoteles Voltaire Federer
Bismarck Vigny Barlach Heine Herodot
Gengenbach
Storm Casanova Tersteegen Grillparzer Georgy
Chamberlain Lessing Langbein Gilm Gryphius
Brentano Lafontaine
Strachwitz Claudius Schiller Kralik Iffland Sokrates
Bellamy Schilling
Katharina II. von Rußland Gerstäcker Raabe Gibbon Tschechow
Löns Hesse Hoffmann Gogol Wilde Gleim Vulpius
Luther Heym Hofmannsthal Klee Hölty Morgenstern
Roth Goedicke
Heyse Klopstock Kleist
Luxemburg Puschkin Homer Mörike
La Roche Horaz Musil
Machiavelli Kierkegaard Kraft Kraus
Navarra Aurel Musset Moltke
Lamprecht Kind Kirchhoff Hugo
Nestroy Marie de France
Laotse Ipsen Liebknecht
Nietzsche Nansen Ringelnatz
Marx
von Ossietzky Lassalle Gorki Klett Leibniz
May Irving
vom Stein Lawrence
Petalozzi Knigge
Platon Kafka
Sachs Pückler Michelangelo Kock
Poe Liebermann Korolenko
de Sade Praetorius Mistral Zetkin

The publishing house tredition has created the series **TREDITION CLASSICS**. It contains classical literature works from over two thousand years. Most of these titles have been out of print and off the bookstore shelves for decades.

The book series is intended to preserve the cultural legacy and to promote the timeless works of classical literature. As a reader of a **TREDITION CLASSICS** book, the reader supports the mission to save many of the amazing works of world literature from oblivion.

The symbol of **TREDITION CLASSICS** is Johannes Gutenberg (1400 – 1468), the inventor of movable type printing.

With the series, tredition intends to make thousands of international literature classics available in printed format again – worldwide.

All books are available at book retailers worldwide in paperback and in hardcover. For more information please visit: www.tredition.com

tredition was established in 2006 by Sandra Latusseck and Soenke Schulz. Based in Hamburg, Germany, tredition offers publishing solutions to authors and publishing houses, combined with worldwide distribution of printed and digital book content. tredition is uniquely positioned to enable authors and publishing houses to create books on their own terms and without conventional manufacturing risks.

For more information please visit: www.tredition.com

De Carmine Pastorali (1684)

René Rapin

Imprint

This book is part of the TREDITION CLASSICS series.

Author: René Rapin
Cover design: toepferschumann, Berlin (Germany)

Publisher: tredition GmbH, Hamburg (Germany)
ISBN: 978-3-8491-4738-9

www.tredition.com
www.tredition.de

INTRODUCTION

Recent students of criticism have usually placed Rapin in the School of Sense. In fact Rapin clearly denominates himself a member of that school. In the introduction to his major critical work, <u>Reflexions sur la Poetique d'Aristote</u> (1674), he states that his essay "is nothing else, but Nature put in Method, and good <u>Sense</u> reduced to Principles" (<u>Reflections on Aristotle's Treatise of Poesie</u>, London, 1731, II, 131). And in a few passages as early as "A Treatise de Carmine Pastorali" (1659), he seems to imply that he is being guided in part at least by the criterion of "good <u>Sense</u>." For example, after citing several writers to prove that "brevity" is one of the "graces" of pastoral poetry, he concludes, "I could heap up a great many more things to this purpose, but I see no need of such a trouble, since no man can rationally doubt of the goodness of my Observation" (p.41).

The basic criterion, nevertheless, which Rapin uses in the "Treatise" is the authority of the Ancients--the poems of Theocritus and Virgil and the criticism of Aristotle and Horace. Because of his constant refer-ences to the Ancients, one is likely to conclude that he (like Boileau and Pope) must have thought they and Nature (good sense) were the same. In a number of passages, however, Rapin depends solely on the Ancients. Two examples will suffice to illustrate his absolutism. At the beginning of "<u>The Second</u> Part," when he is inquiring "into the nature of <u>Pastoral,</u>" he admits:
And this must needs be a hard Task, since I have no guide, neither <u>Aristotle</u> nor <u>Horace</u> to direct me.... And I am of opinion that none can treat well and clearly of any kind of <u>Poetry</u> if he hath no helps from these two (p. 16).
In "<u>The Third</u> Part," when he begins to "lay down" his <u>Rules for writing</u> Pastorals," he declares:
iiYet in this difficulty I will follow <u>Aristotle</u>'s Example, who being to lay down Rules concerning <u>Epicks,</u> propos'd <u>Homer</u> as a Pattern, from whom he deduc'd the whole Art; So I will gather from <u>Theocritus</u> and <u>Virgil</u>, those Fathers of <u>Pastoral</u>, what I shall deliver on this account (p. 52).

These passages represent the apogee of the neoclassical criticism of pastoral poetry. No other critic who wrote on the pastoral depends so completely on the authority of the classical critics and poets. As a matter of fact, Rapin himself is not so absolute later. In the section of the _Réflexions_ on the pastoral, he merely states that the best models are Theocritus and Virgil. In short, one may say that in the "Treatise" the influence of the Ancients is dominant; in the _Réflexions_, "good _Sense_."

Reduced to its simplest terms, Rapin's theory is Virgilian. When deducing his theory from the works of Theocritus and Virgil, his preference is almost without exception for Virgil. Finding Virgil's eclogues refined and elegant, Rapin, with a suggestion from Donatus (p. 10 and p. 14), concludes that the pastoral "belongs properly to the _Golden Age_" (p. 37)--"that blessed time, when Sincerity and Innocence, Peace, Ease, and Plenty inhabited the Plains" (p. 5). Here, then, is the immediate source of the Golden Age eclogue, which, being transferred to England and popularised by Pope, flourished until the time of Dr. Johnson and Joseph Warton.

In France the most prominent opponent to the theory formulated by Rapin is Fontenelle. In his "Discours sur la Nature de l'Eglogue" (1688) Fontenelle, with studied and impertinent disregard for the Ancients and for "ceux qui professent cette espèce de religion que l'on s'est faite d'adorer l'antiquité," expressly states that the basic criterion by which he worked was "les lumières naturelles de la raison" (_OEuvres_, Paris, 1790, V, 36). It is careless and incorrect to imply that Rapin's and Fontenelle's theories of pastoral poetry are similar, as Pope, Joseph Warton, and many other critics and scholars haveiii done. Judged by basic critical principles, method, or content there is a distinct difference between Rapin and Fontenelle. Rapin is primarily a neoclassicist in his "Treatise"; Fontenelle, a rationalist in his "Discours." It is this opposition, then, of neoclassicism and rationalism, that constitutes the basic issue of pastoral criticism in England during the Restoration and the early part of the eighteenth century.

When Fontenelle's "Discours" was translated in 1695, the first phrase of it quoted above was translated as "those Pedants who profess a kind of Religion which consists of worshipping the Ancients" (p. 294). Fontenelle's phrase more nearly than that of the English translator describes Rapin. Though Rapin's erudition was great, he escaped the quagmire of pedantry. He refers most frequently to the scholiasts and editors in "<u>The First Part</u>" (which is so trivial that one wonders why he ever troubled to accumulate so much insignificant material), but after quoting them he does not hesitate to call their ideas "pedantial" (p. 24) and to refer to their statements as grammarian's "prattle" (p. 11). And, though at times it seems that his curiosity and industry impaired his judgment, Rapin does draw significant ideas from such scholars and critics as Quintilian, Vives, Scaliger, Donatus, Vossius, Servius, Minturno, Heinsius, and Salmasius.

Rapin's most prominent disciple in England is Pope. Actually, Pope presents no significant idea on this subject that is foreign to Rapin, and much of the language--terminology and set phrases--of Pope's "Discourse" comes directly from Rapin's "Treatise" and from the section on the pastoral in the <u>Reflections</u>. Contrary to his own statement that he "reconciled" some points on which the critics disagree and in spite of the fact that he quotes Fontenelle, Pope in his "Discourse" is a neoclassicist almost as thoroughgoing as Rapin. ivThe ideas which he says he took from Fontenelle are either unimportant or may be found in Rapin. Pope ends his "Discourse" by drawing a general conclusion concerning his <u>Pastorals</u>: "But after all, if they have any merit, it is to be attributed to some good old authors, whose works as I had leisure to study, so I have not wanted care to imitate." This statement is diametrically opposed to the basic ideas and methods of Fontenelle, but in full accord with and no doubt directly indebted to those of Rapin.

The same year, 1717, that Pope 'imitated' Rapin's "Treatise," Thomas Purney made a direct attack on Rapin's neoclassic procedure. In the "Preface" to his own <u>Pastorals</u> he expresses his disapproval of Rapin's method, evidently with the second passage from Rapin quoted above in mind:
<u>Rapine's</u> Discourse is counted the best on this Poem, for 'tis the longest. You will easily excuse my not mentioning all his Defects and Errors

in this Preface. I shall only say then, that instead of looking into the true Nature of the Pastoral Poem, and then judging whether <u>Theocritus</u> or any of his Followers have brought it to it's utmost Perfection or not. <u>Rapine</u> takes it for granted that <u>Theocritus</u> and <u>Virgil</u> are infallible; and aim's at nothing beyond showing the Rules which he thinks they observ'd. Facetious Head! (<u>Works</u>, Oxford, 1933, pp. 51-52. The Peroy Reprints, No. XII)

The influence of Rapin on the development of the pastoral, nevertheless, was salutary. Finding the genre vitiated with wit, extravagance, and artificiality, he attempted to strip it of these Renaissance excrescencies and restore it to its pristine purity by direct reference to the Ancients--Virgil, in particular. Though Rapin does not have the psychological insight into the esthetic principles of the genre equal to that recently exhibited by William Empson or even to that expressed by Fontenelle, he does understand the intrinsic appeal of the pastoral which has enabled it to survive, and often to flourish, through the centuries in painting, music, andv poetry. Perhaps his most explicit expression of this appreciation is made while he is discussing Horace's statement that the muses love the country:

And to speak from the very bottome of my heart... methinks he is much more happy in a Wood, that at ease contemplates this universe, as his own, and in it, the Sun and Stars, the pleasing Meadows, shady Groves, green Banks, stately Trees, flowing Springs, and the wanton windings of a River, fit objects for quiet innocence, than he that with Fire and Sword disturbs the World, and measures his possessions by the wast that lys about him (p. 4).

René Rapin (1621-1687), in spite of his duties as a Jesuit priest and disputes with the Jansenists, became one of the most widely read men of his time and carried on the celebrated discussions about the Ancients with Maimbourg and Vavasseur. His <u>chef-d'oeuvre</u> without contradiction is <u>Hortorum libri IV</u>. Like Virgil, Spenser, Pope, and many aspiring lesser poets, he began his literary career by writing pastorals, <u>Eclogae Sacrae</u> (1659), to which is prefixed in Latin the original of "A Treatise de Carmine Pastorali."

   J.E. Congleton

University of Florida

Reprinted here from the copy owned by the Boston Athenaeum by permission.

1

A

TREATISE

de CARMINE PASTORALI

Written by RAPIN.

The First Part.

TO be as short as possible in my discourse upon the present Subject, I shall not touch upon the Excellency of *Poetry* in general; nor repeat those high *Encomiums*, (as that tis the most divine of all human Arts, and the like) which *Plato* in his *Jone*, *Aristotele* in his *Poetica*, and other Learned men have copiously insisted on: And this I do that I might more closely and briefly pursue my present design, which, no doubt will not please every man; for since I treat of that part of *Poetry*, which (to use *Quintilian's* words,) by reason of its Clownishness, is affraid of the Court and City; some may imagine that I follow *Nichocaris* his humor, who would paint only the most ugly and deform'd, and those too in the meanest and most frightful dress, that real, or fancy'd Poverty could put them in.

2For some think that to be a Sheapard is in it self mean, base, and sordid; And this I think is the first thing that the graver and soberer sort will be ready to object.

But if we consider how honorable that employment is, our Objectors from that Topick will be easily answer'd, for as *Heroick* Poems owe their dignity to the Quality of *Heroes*, so *Pastorals* to that of *Sheapards*.

Now to manifest this, I shall not rely on the authority of the *Fabulous*, and *Heroick* Ages, tho, in the former, a God fed Sheep in *Thessaly*, and in the latter, *Hercules* the Prince of *Heroes*, (as *Paterculus* stiles him) graz'd on mount *Aventine*: These Examples, tis true, are not convinceing, yet they sufficiently shew that the employment of a Sheapard was sometime look'd upon to be such, as in those Fabulous times was not alltogether unbecomeing the *Dignity* of a *Heroe*, or the *Divinity* of a *God*: which consideration if it cannot be of force enough to procure excellence, yet certainly it may secure it from the imputation of baseness, since it was sometime lookt upon as fit for the greatest in Earth or Heaven.

But not to insist on the authority of *Poets*, *Sacred Writt* tells us that *Jacob* and *Esau*, two great men, were Sheapards; And *Amos*, one of the Royal Family, asserts the same of himself, for *He was* among *the Sheapards of Tecua*, following that employment: The like by Gods own appoint3ment prepared *Moses* for a Scepter, as *Philo* intimates in his life, when He tells us, *that a Sheapards Art is a suitable preparation to a Kingdome*; the same He mentions in the Life of *Joseph*, affirming that the care a Sheapard hath over his Cattle, very much resembles that which a King hath over his Subjects: The same *Basil* in his Homily de *S. Mamm. Martyre* hath concerning *David*, who was taken from following the Ews great with young ones to feed *Israel*, for He says that the Art of feeding and governing are very near akin, and even Sisters: And upon this account I suppose twas, that Kings amongst the *Greeks* reckoned the name of Sheapard one of their greatest titles, for, if we believe *Varro*, amongst the Antients, the best and bravest was still a Sheapard: Every body knows that the *Romans* the worthiest and greatest Nation in the World sprang from *Sheapards*: The Augury of the Twelve Vulturs plac't a Scepter in *Romulus*'s hand which held a Crook before; and at that time, as *Ovid* says,

His own small Flock each Senator did keep.

Lucretius mentions an extraordinary happiness, and as it were Divinity in a *Sheaperd's* life,

Thro Sheapards ease, and their Divine retreats.

And this is the reason, I suppose, why the solitude of the Country, the shady Groves, and security of that happy Quiet was so grateful to the Muses, for thus *Horace* represents them,

4
The Muses that the Country Love.

Which Observation was first made by *Mnasalce* the *Sicyonian* in his Epigram upon *Venus*

The Rural Muse upon the Mountains feeds.

For sometimes the Country is so raveshing and delightful, that twill raise Wit and Spirit even in the dullest Clod, And in truth, amongst so many heats of Lust and Ambition which usually fire our Citys, I cannot see what retreat, what comfort is left for a chast and sober Muse.

And to speak from the very bottome of my heart, (not to mention the integrity and innocence of Sheapards upon which so many have insisted, and so copiously declaimed) methinks he is much more happy in a Wood, that at ease contemplates this universe, as his own, and in it, the Sun and Stars, the pleasing Meadows, shady Groves, green Banks, stately Trees, flowing Springs, and the wanton windings of a River, fit objects for quiet innocence, than he that with Fire and Sword disturbs the World, and measures his possessions by the wast that lys about him: *Augustus* in the remotest East fights for peace, but how tedious were his Voyages? how troublesome his Marches? how great his disquiets? what fears and hopes distracted his designs? whilst *Tityrus* contented with a little, happy in the enjoyment of his Love, and at ease under his spreading Beech.

Taught Trees to sound his Amaryllis *name.*

5 On the one side *Meliboeus* is forc't to leave his Country, and *Antony* on the other; the one a Sheapard, the other a great man, in the Common-Wealth; how disagreeable was the Event? the Sheapard could endure himself; and sit down contentedly under his misfortunes, whilst lost *Antony,*unable to hold out, and quitting all hopes both for himself and his Queen, became his own barbarous Executioner: Than which sad and deplorable fall I cannot imagine what could be worse, for certainly nothing is so miserable as a Wretch made so from a flowrishing & happy man; by which tis evident how much we ought to prefer before the gaity of a great and shining State, that Idol of the Crowd, the lowly simplicity of a Sheapards Life: for what is that but a perfect image of the state of Innocence, of that golden Age, that blessed time, when Sincerity and Innocence, Peace, Ease, and Plenty inhabited the Plains?

Take the Poets description

Here Lowly Innocence makes a sure retreat,
A harmless Life, and ignorant of deceit,
and free from fears with various sweet's encrease,
And all's or'e spread with the soft wings of Peace:
Here Oxen low, here Grots, and purling Streams,
And Spreading shades invite to easy dreams.

And thus *Horace,*

Happy the man beyond pretence
Such was the state of Innocence, &c.

6 And from this head I think the dignity of *Bucolicks* is sufficiently cleared, for as much as the Golden Age is to be preferred before the *Heroick,* so much *Pastorals* must excell *Heroick* Poems: yet this is so to be understood, that if we look upon the majesty and loftiness of *Heroick* Poems, it must be confest that they justly claim the preheminence; but if the unaffected neatness, elegant, graceful smartness of the expression, or the polite dress of a Poem be considered, then they fall short of *Pastorals:* for this sort flows with Sweet, Elegant, neat and pleasing fancies; as is too evident to every one that hath tasted the sweeter muses, to need a farther explication: for tis not probable that *Asinius Pollio, Cinna, Varius, Cornelius Gallus,* men of the neatest Wit, and that lived in the most polite Age, or that *Augustus Cæsar* the Prince of the *Roman* elegance, as well as of the common Wealth, should be so extreamly taken with *Virgils Bucolicks,* or that *Virgil* himself a man of such singular prudence, and so correct a judgment, should dedicate his Eclogues to those great Persons; unless he had known that there is somewhat more then ordinary Elegance in those sort of Composures, which the wise perceive, tho far above the understanding of the Crowd: nay if *Ludovicus Vives,* a very learned man, and admired for politer studies may be believed, there is somewhat more sublime and excellent in those *Pastorals,* than the Common 7 sort of Grammarians imagine: This I shall discourse of in an other place, and now inquire into the Antiquity of Pastorals.

The Antiquity of Pastorals.

Since *Linus*, *Orpheus*, and *Eumolpus* were famous for their Poems, before the *Trojan* wars; those are certainly mistaken, who date Poetry from that time; I rather incline to their opinion who make it as old as the World it self; which Assertion as it ought to be understood of Poetry in general, so especially of *Pastoral*, which, as *Scaliger* delivers, was the most antient kind of Poetry, and resulting from the most *antient* way of Liveing: *Singing first began amongst Sheapards as they fed their Flocks, either by the impulse of nature, or in imitation of the notes of Birds, or the whispering of Trees.*

For since the first men were either *Sheapards* or *Ploughmen*, and *Sheapards*, as may be gathered out of *Thucydides* and *Varro*, were before the others, they were the first that either invited by their leisure, or (which *Lucretius* thinks more probable) in imitation of Birds, began a tune.

Thro all the Woods they heard the pleasing noise
Of chirping Birds, and try'd to frame their voice,
And Imitate, thus Birds instructed man,
And taught them Songs before their Art began.

In short, tis so certain that Verses first began in the Country that the thing is in it self evident, and this *Tibullus* very plainly signifies,

8
First weary at his Plough the labouring Hind
In certain feet his rustick words did bind:
His dry reed first he tun'd at sacred feasts
To thanks the bounteous Gods, and cheer his Guests.

In certain feet according to *Bern Cylenius* of *Verona* his interpretation *in set measures*: for *Censorinus* tells us, that the antient Songs were loose and not ty'd up to any strict numbers, and afterwards by certain laws and acknowledged rules were confin'd to such and such measures: for this is the method of Nature in all her works, from imperfect and rude beginnings things take their first rise, and afterwards by fit and apposite additions are polish't, and brought to perfection: such were the Verses which heretofore the *Italian* Sheapards and Plough-men, as *Virgil* says, sported amongst themselves.

Italian Plough-men sprung from antient Troy
Did sport unpolish't Rhymes----

Lucretius in his Fifth Book *de Natura Rerum*, says, that Sheapards were first taught by the rushing of soft Breezes amongst the Canes to blow their Reeds, and so by degrees to put their Songs in tune.

For Whilst soft Evening Gales blew or'e the Plains
And shook the sounding Reeds, they taught the Swains,
And thus the Pipe was fram'd, and tuneful Reed,
And whilst the Flocks did then securely feed,
The harmless Sheapards tun'd their Pipes to Love,
And Amaryllis name fill'd every Grove.
9

From all which tis very plain that *Poetry* began in those days, when Sheapards took up their employment: to this agrees *Donatus* in his Life of *Virgil*, and *Pontanus* in his Fifth Book of Stars, as appears by these Verses.

Here underneath a shade by purling Springs
The Sheapards Dance, whilst sweet Amyntas *sings;*
Thus first the new found Pipe was tun'd to Love,
And Plough-men taught their Sweet hearts to the Grove,

Thus the *Fescennine* jests when they sang harvest-home, and then too the Grape gatherers and Reapers Songs began, an elegant example of which we have in the Tenth *Idyllium* of *Theocritus*.

From this birth, as it were, of *Poetry*, Verse began to grow up to greater matters; For from the common discourse of *Plough-men* and *Sheapards*, first *Comedy*, that Mistress of a private Life, next *Tragedy*, and then *Epick Poetry* which is lofty and *Heroical* arrose, This *Maximus Tyrius* confirms in his Twenty first dissertation, where he tells us that Plough-men just comeing from their work, and scarce cleansed from the filth of their employment, did use to flurt out some sudden and *extempore* Catches; and from this beginning Plays were produc'd and the Stage erected: Thus 10 much concerning the *Antiquity*, next of the *Original* of this sort.

About this Learned men cannot agree, for who was the first Author, is not sufficiently understood; *Donatus*, tis true, tells us tis proper to the Golden Age, and therefore must needs be the product of that happy time: but who was the Author, where, what time it was first invented hath been a great Controversy, and not yet sufficiently determined: *Epicharmus* one of *Pythagoras* his School, in his alkyoni mentions one *Diomus* a *Sicilian*, who, if we believe *Athænæus* was the first that wrote *Pastorals: those that fed Cattle had a peculiar kind of Poetry, call'd Bucolicks, of which Dotimus a Sicilian was inventer:*

*Diodorus Siculus*en tois mythologoumenois, seems to make *Daphnis* the son of *Mercury* and a certain *Nymph*, to be the Author; and agreeable to this, *Theon* an old *scholiast* on *Theocritus*, in his notes upon the first *Idyllium* mentioning *Daphnis*, adds, *he was the author of Bucolicks*, and *Theocritus himself* calls him *the Muses Darling*: and to this Opinion of *Diodorus Siculus Polydore Virgil* readily assents.

But *Mnaseas* of *Patara* in a discourse of his concerning *Europa*, speaks thus of a Son of *Pan* the God of Sheapards: *Panis Filium Bubulcum à quo & Bucolice canere:* Now Whether *Mnaseas* by that *Bubulcum*, means only a *Herds-man*, or one skilled in *Bucolicks*, is uncertain; but if *Valla's*11 judgment be good, tis to be taken of the latter: yet *Ælian* was of another mind, for he boldly affirms that *Stesichorus* called *Himeræus* was the first, and in the same place adds, that *Daphnis* the Son of *Mercury* was the first Subject of *Bucolicks*.

Some ascribe the Honor to *Bacchus* the President of the *Nymphs, Satyrs*, and the other Country Gods, perhaps because he delighted in the Country; and others attribute it to *Apollo* called *Nomius* the God of Sheapards, and that he invented it then when he served *Admetus* in *Thessaly*, and fed his Herds: For, tis likely, he to recreate himself, and pass away his time, applied his mind to such Songs as were best suitable to his present condition: Many think we owe it to *Pan* the God of Sheapards, not a few to *Diana* that extreamly delighted in solitude and Woods; and some say *Mercury* himself: of all which whilst *Grammarians* prattle, according to their usual custome they egregiously trifle; they suffer themselves to be put upon by Fables, and resign their judgment up to foolish pretentions, but things and solid truth is that we seek after.

As about the Author, so concerning the place of its Birth there is a great dispute, some say *Sparta*, others *Peloponesus*, but most are for *Sicily*.

Valla the Placentine, a curious searcher into Antiquity, thinks this sort of Poetry first appear'd amongst the *Lacedemonians*, for when the *Persians* had wasted allmost all *Greece*, the *Spartans* say 12 that they for fear of the *Barbarians* fled into Caves and lurking holes; and that the Country Youth then began to apply themselves in Songs to *Diana Caryatis*, together with the Maids, who midst their Songs of-ferd Flowers to the Goddess: which custome containing somewhat of Religion was in those places a long time very scrupulously ob-served.

Diomedes the Grammarian, in his treatise of *Measures*, declares *Sicily* to be the Place: for thus he says, the *Sicilian* Sheapards in time of a great *Pestilence*, began to invent new Ceremonies to appease in-censed *Diana*, whom afterward, for affording her help, and stopping the Plague they called Lyên: *i.e.* the *Freer* from their Miserys. This grew into custom, and the Sheapards used to meet in Companies, to sing their deliverer *Diana's* praise, and these afterwards passing into *Italy* were there named *Bucoliastæ*.

Pomponius Sabinus tells the story thus: When the Hymns the Vir-gins us'd to sing in the Country to *Diana* were left off, because, by reason of the present Wars, the Maidens were forc't to keep close within the Towns; the Shepherds met, and sang these kind of Songs, which are now call'd *Bucolicks*, to *Diana*; to whom they could not give the usual worship by reason of the Wars: But *Donatus* says, that this kind of Verses was first sung to *Diana* by *Orestes*, when he wandred about *Italy*; after he fled from *Scythia Taurica*, and had 13 taken away the Image of the Goddess and hid it in a bundle of sticks, whence she receiv'd the name of *Fascelina*, or *Phacelide*apo tou phakelou At whose Altar, the very same *Orestes* was afterward ex-piated by his Sister *Iphigenia*: But how can any one rely on such Fables, when the inconsiderable Authors that propose them disa-gree so much amongst themselves?

Some are of Opinion that the Shepherds, were wont in solem and set Songs about the Fields and Towns to celebrate the Goddess *Pales*; and beg her to bless their flocks and fields with a plenteous encrease and that from hence the name, and composure of *Bucolicks* continued.

Other prying ingenious Men make other conjectures, as to this mazing Controversy thus *Vossius* delivers himself; *The Antients cannot be reconcil'd, but I rather incline to their opinion who think* Bucol-icks *were invented either by the* Sicilians *or* Peloponesians, *for both those use the* Dorick *dialect, and all the* Greek Bucolicks *are writ in that*:

As for my self I think, that what *Horace* says of *Elegies* may be apply'd to the present Subject.

But who soft Elegies was the first that wrote
Grammarians doubt, and cannot end the doubt:

For I find nothing certain about this matter, since neither *Valla* a diligent inquirer after, and a good judge in such things, nor any of the late writers produce any thing upon which I can safely rely; yet what beginning this kind of Poetry 14 had, I think I can pretty well conjecture: for tis likely that first Shepherds us'd Songs to recreate themselves in their leisure hours whilst they fed their Sheep; and that each man, as his wit served, accommodated his Songs to his present Circumstances: to this Solitude invited, and the extream leisure that attends that employment absolutely requir'd it: For as their retirement gave them leisure, and Solitude a fit place for Meditation, Meditation and Invention produc'd a Verse; which is nothing else but a Speech fit to be sung, and so Songs began: Thus *Hesiod* was made a Poet, for he acknowledges himself that he receiv'd his inspiration;

Whilst under Helicon *he fed his Lambs.*

for either the leisure or fancy of Shepherds seems to have a natural aptitude to Verse.

And indeed I cannot but agree with *Lucretius* that accurate Searcher into Nature, who delivers that from that state of Innocence the Golden Age, Pastorals continued down to his time, for after he had in his fifth book describ'd that most happy age, he adds,

For then the Rural Muses reign'd.

From whence 'tis very plain, that as *Donatus* himself observ'd, Pastorals were the invention of the simplicity and innocence of that Golden age, if there was ever any such, or certainly of that time which succeeded the beginning of the World: For tho the Golden Age must be ac15knowledged to be only in the fabulous times, yet 'tis certain that the Manners of the first Men were so plain and simple, that we may easily derive both the innocent imployment of Shepherds, and Pastorals from them.

16

The Second PART.

NOW let us inquire into the nature of *Pastoral*, in what its excellencies consist, and how it must be made to be exact: And this must needs be a hard Task, since I have no guide, neither *Aristotle* nor *Horace* to direct me; for both they, whatever was the matter, speak not one word of this sort of Verse. And I am of opinion that none can treat well and clearly of any kind of *Poetry* if he hath no helps from these two: But since they lay down some general Notions of *Poetry* which may be useful in the present case, I shall follow their steps as close as possible I can.

Not only *Aristotle* but *Horace* too hath defin'd that *Poetry* in general is Imitation; I mention only these two, for tho *Plato* in his Second Book *de Rep.* and in his *Timæus* delivers the same thing, I shall not make use of his Authority at all: Now as *Comedy* according to *Aristotle* is the *Image and Representation of a gentiel and City Life*, so is *Pastoral Poetry* of a County and *Sheapards* Life; for since *Poetry* in general is Imitation; its several *Species* must likewise Imitate, take *Aristotles* own words *Cap.* 1. pasai tynchanousin ousa mimêseis; And these *Species* are 17 differenc't either by the subject matter, when the things to be imitated are quite different, or when the manner in which you imitate, or the mode of imitation is so: en trisi dê tautais diaphorais hê mimêsis estin, en hois kai ha, kai hôs: Thus tho of *Epick* Poetry and *Tragedy* the Subject is the same, and some great illustrious Action is to be *imitated* by both, yet since one by representation, and the other by plain narration imitates, each makes a different *Species* of imitation. And *Comedy* and *Tragedy*, tho they agree in this, that both represent, yet because the Matter is different, and *Tragedy* must represent some brave action, and *Comedy* a humor; these Two sorts of imitation are *Specifically different*. And upon the same account, since *Pastoral* chooses the manners of Sheapards for its imitation, it takes from its matter a peculiar difference, by which it is distinguish'd frõ all others.

But here *Benius* in his comments upon *Aristotle* hath started a considerable query: which is this; Whether *Aristotle*, when he reckons up the different *Species* of Poetry *Cap* 1. doth include *Pastoral,* or no? And about this I find learn'd men cannot at all agree: which certainly *Benius* should have determin'd, or not rais'd: some refer it to that sort which *was sung to Pipes*, for that *Pastorals* were so *Apuleius* intimates, when at the marriage Feast of *Phyche* He brings in *Paniscus* singing *Bucolicks* to his Pipe; But since they did not seriously enough consider, what *Aristotle*18 meant by that which he calls aulêtikên they trifle, talk idly, and are not to be heeded in this matter; For suppose some *Musitian* should sing *Virgils Ænæis* to the Harp, (and *Ant. Lullus* says it hath been done,) should we therefore reckon that divine and incomparable Master of *Heroick* Poetry amongst the *Lyricks*?

Others with *Cæsius Bassus* and *Isacius Tzetzes* hold that that distribution of *Poetry*, which *Aristotle* and *Tully* hath left us, is deficient and imperfect; and that only the chief Species are reckoned, but the more inconsiderable not mention'd: I shall not here interest my self in that quarrel of the *Criticks*, whether we have all *Aristotles* books of Poetry or no; this is a considerable difficulty I confess, for *Laertius* who accurately weighs this matter, says that he wrote two books of *Poetry*, the one lost, and the other we have, tho *Mutinensis* is of an other mind: but to end this dispute, I must agree with *Vossius*, who says the Philosopher comprehended these Species not expressly mentioned, under a higher and more noble head: and that therefore *Pastoral* was contain'd in *Epick.* for these are his own words, *besides there are Epicks of an inferior rank, such as the Writers of Bucolicks. Sincerus*, as *Minturnus* quotes him, is of the same mind, for thus he delivers his opinion concerning *Epick Verse*: *The matters about which these numbers may be employed is various; either mean and low, as in Pastorals, great and lofty, as when 19 the Subject is Divine Things, or Heroick Actions, or of a middle rank, as when we use them to deliver precepts in:* And this likewise he signifys before, where he sets down three sorts of *Epicks: one of which, says he, is divine, and the most excellent by much in all Poetry; the other the lowest but most pure, in which Theocritus excelled, which indeed shews nothing of Poetry beside the bare numbers*: These points being thus settled, the remaining difficultys will be more easily dispatched.

For as in *Dramatick* Poetry the Dignity and meanness of the *Persons* represented make two different *Species of imitation* the one *Tragick*, which agrees to none but great and Illustrious persons, the other *Comick*, which suits with common and gentile humors: so in *Epick* too, there may be reckoned two sorts of *Imitation*, one of which belongs to *Heroes*, and that makes the *Heroick*; the other to *Rusticks* and *Sheapards* and that constitutes the *Pastoral*, now as a *Picture* imitates the Features of the face, so *Poetry* doth action, and tis not a representation of the Person but the Action. *The Definition of Pastoral.* From all which we may gather this definition of Pastoral: *It is the imitation of the Action of a Sheapard, or of one taken under that Character*: Thus *Virgil's Gallus*, tho not really a *Sheapard*, for he was a man of great quality in *Rome*, yet belongs to *Pastoral*, because he is represented like a Sheapard: hence the Poet:

20
The Goatherd and the heavy Heardsmen came,
And ask't what rais'd the deadly Flame.

The *Scene* lys amongst Sheapards, the *Swains* are brought in, the *Herdsmen* come to see his misery, and the fiction is suited to the real condition of a *Sheapard*; the same is to be said for his *Silenus*, who tho he seems lofty, and to sound to loud for an oaten reed, yet since what he sings he sings to *Sheapards*, and suits his Subject to their apprehensions, his is to be acknowledged *Pastoral*. This rule we must stick to, that we might infallibly discern what is stricktly *Pastoral* in *Virgil* and *Theocritus*, and what not: for in *Theocritus* there are some more lofty thoughts which not having any thing belonging to Sheapards for their Subject, must by no means be accounted *Pastoral*, But of this more in its proper place.

My present inquiry must be what is the *Subject Matter* of a *Pastoral*, about which it is not easy to resolve; since neither from *Aristotle*, nor any of the *Greeks* who have written *Pastorals*, we can receive certain direction. For sometimes they treat of high and sublime things, like *Epick Poets*; what can be loftier than the whole *Seaventh Idyllium of Bias* in which *Myrsan* urges *Lycidas* the Sheapard to sing the Loves of *Deidamia* and *Achilles*. For he begins from *Helen's* rape, and goes on to the revengful fury of the *Atrides*, and shuts up in one *Pastoral*, all that is great and sounding in *Homers Iliad*.

21
Sparta was fir'd with Rage
And gather'd Greece to prosecute Revenge.

And *Theocritus* his verses are sometimes as sounding and his thoughts as high: for upon serious consideration I cannot mind what part of all the *Heroicks* is so strong and sounding as that *Idylli-um* on *Hercules*leontophonô in which *Hercules* himself tells *Phyleus* how he kill'd the Lyon whose Skin he wore: for, not to mention many, what can be greater than this expression.

And gaping Hell received his mighty Soul:

Why should I instance in the dioskouroi, which hath not one line below Heroick; the greatness of this is almost inexpressible.

anêr hyperoplos enêmeros, endiaaske
deinos idein

And some other pieces are as strong as these, such is the *Panegyrick on Ptolemy, Helen's Epithalamium*, and the Fight of young *Hercules* and the Snakes: now how is it likely that such Subjects should be fit for *Pastorals*, of which in my opinion, the same may be said which *Ovid* doth of his *Cydippe*.

Cydippe, Homer, doth not fit thy Muse.

For certainly *Pastorals* ought not to rise to the Majesty of *Heroicks*: but who on the other side 22 dares reprehend such great and judicious Authors, whose very doing it is Authority enough? What shall I say of *Virgil*? who in his Sixth *Eclogue* hath put together allmost all the particulars of the fabulous Age; what is so high to which *Silenus* that Master of Mysterys doth not soar?

For lo! he sung the Worlds stupendious birth,
How scatter'd seeds of sea, of Air, and Earth,
And purer Fire thro universal night
And empty space did fruitfully unite:
From whence th' innumerable race of things
By circular successive order springs.

And afterward

How Pyrra's Stony race rose from the ground,
And Saturn reign'd with Golden plenty crown'd,
How bold Prometheus *(whose untam'd desire,*
Rival'd the Sun with his own Heavenly Fire)
Now doom'd the Scythian *Vulturs endless prey*
Severely pays for Animating Clay:

So true, so certain 'tis, that nothing is so high and lofty to which *Bucolicks* may not successfully aspire. But if this be so, what will become of *Macrobius, Georgius Valla, Julius Scaliger, Vossius,* and the whole company of Grammarians? who all affirm that simplicity and meanness is so essential to *Pastorals*, that it ought to be confin'd to the State, Manners, Apprehension and even common phrases of Sheapards: for nothing can 23 be said to be *Pastoral*, which is not accommodated to their condition; and for this Reason *Nannius Alcmaritanus* in my opinion is a trifler, who, in his comments on *Virgils Eclogues*, thinks that those sorts of Composures may now and then be lofty, and treat of great subjects: where he likewise divides the matter of *Bucolicks*, into *Low, Middle,* and *High*: and makes *Virgil* the Author of this Division, who in his Fourth *Eclogue*, (as he imagines) divides the matter of *Bucolicks* into Three sorts, and intimates this division by these three words: *Bushes, Shrubs* and *Woods*.

Sicilian Muse begin a loftier strain,
The Bushes and the Shrubs that shade the Plain
Delight not all; if I to Woods repair
My Song shall make them worth a Consuls Care.

By Woods, as he fancys, as *Virgil* means high and stately Trees, so He would have a great and lofty Subject to to be implyed,such as he designed for the *Consul*: by Bushes, which are almost even with the ground, the meanest and lowest argument; and by Shrubs a Subject not so high as the one, nor so low as the other, as the thing it-self is, And therefore these lines

If I to Woods repair
My Song shall make them worth a Consuls *care.*

24 are thus to be understood, That if we choose high and sublime arguments, our work will be fit for the Patronage of a *Consul*, This is *Nanniu's* interpretation of that place; too pedantial and subtle I'me affraid, for tis not credible that ever *Virgil* thought of reckoning great and lofty things amongst the Subjects of *Bucolicks* especially since

When his Thalia *rais'd her bolder voice*
And Kings and Battles were her lofty choice,
Phæbus *did twitch his Ear, mean thoughts infuse,*
And with this whisper check't th' inspiring Muse.

A Sheapard, Tityrus, his Sheep should feed,
And choose a subject suited to his reed,

This certainly was a serious admonition, implyed by the twitching of his Ear, and I believe if he had continued in this former humor and not obey'd the smarting admonition. He had still felt it: so far was he from thinking Kings and Battels fit Themes for a *Sheapards* song: and this evidently shows that in *Virgils* opinion, contrary to *Nanniu's* fancy, great things cannot in the least be comprehended within the subject matter of *Pastorals;* no, it must be low and humble, which *Theocritus* very happily expresseth by this word Boukoli-asdên*i. e.* as the interpreters explain it, sing humble Strains.

Therefore let *Pastoral* never venture upon a 25 lofty subject, let it not recede one jot from its proper matter, but be employ'd about Rustick affairs: such as are mean and humble in themselves; and such are the affairs of Shepherds, especially their Loves, but those must be pure and innocent; not disturb'd by vain suspitious jealousy, nor polluted by Rapes; The Rivals must not fight, and their emulations must be without quarrellings: such as *Vida* meant.

Whilst on his Reed he Shepherd's strifes conveys,
And soft complaints in smooth Sicilian lays.

To these may be added *sports, Jests, Gifts,* and *Presents;* but not *costly,* such are yellow Apples, young stock-Doves, Milk, Flowers, and the like; all things must appear delightful and easy, nothing vitious and rough: A perfidious Pimp, a designing Jilt, a gripeing Usurer, a crafty factious Servant must have no room there, but every part must be full of the simplicity of the *Golden-Age,* and of that Candor which was then eminent: for as *Juvenal affirms*

Baseness was a great wonder in that Age;

Sometimes *Funeral-Rites* are the subject of an *Eclogue,* where the Shepherds scatter flowers on the Tomb, and sing Rustick Songs in honor of the Dead: Examples of this kind are left us by *Virgil* in his *Daphnis,* and *Bion* in his *Adonis,* and this hath nothing disagreeable to a Shepherd: In 26 short whatever, the decorum being still preserv'd, can be done by a *Sheapard,* may be the Subject of a *Pastoral.*

Now there may be more kinds of Subjects than *Servius* or *Donatus* allow, for they confine us to that Number which *Virgil* hath made use of, tho *Minturnus* in his second Book *de Poetâ* declares against this opinion: But as a glorious *Heroick* action must be the Subject of an *Heroick* Poem, so a *Pastoral* action of a *Pastoral*; at least it must be so turn'd and wrought, that it might appear to be the action of a *Shepherd*; which caution is very necessary to be observ'd, to clear a great many difficulties in this matter: for tho as the Interpreters assure us; most of *Virgils* Eclogues are about the Civil war, planting Colonys, the murder of the Emperor, and the like, which in themselves are too great and too lofty for humble *Pastoral* to reach, yet because they are accomodated to the Genius of Shepherds, may be the Subject of an *Eclogue*, for that sometimes will admit of Gods and Heroes so they appear like, and are shrouded under the Persons of Shepherds: But as for these matters which neither really are, nor are so wrought as to seem the actions of Shepherds, such are in *Moschus's Europa, Theocritus's Epithalamium of Helen*, and *Virgil's Pollio*, to declare my opinion freely, I cannot think them to be fit Subjects for *Bucolicks*: And upon this account I suppose 'tis that *Servius* in his 27 Comments on *Virgil's Bucoliks* reckons only seven of *Virgil's* ten Eclogues, and onely ten of *Theocritus's* thirty, to be pure Pastorals, and *Salmasius* upon *Solinus* says, that *amongst Theocritus's Poems there are some which you may call what you please Beside Pastorals*: and *Heinsius* in his *Scholia* upon *Theocritus* will allow but Ten of his *Idylliums* to be *Bucoliks*, 1. 2. 3. 4. 5. 6. 7. 8. 9. 11. for all the rest are deficient either in matter or form, and from this number of pure pastoral *Idylliums* I am apt to think, that *Theocritus* seems to have made that Pipe, on which he tun'd his *Pastorals* and which he consecrated to *Pan* of ten Reeds, as *Salmasius* in his notes on *Theocritus's* Pipe hath learnedly observed: *in which two Verses always make one Reed of the Pipe, therefore all are so unequal, like the unequal Reeds of a Pipe, that if you put two equals together which make one Reed, the whole inequality consists in ten pairs*; when in the common Pipes there were usually no more then seven Reeds, and this the less curious observers have heedlessly past by.

Some are of opinion that whatever is done in the Country, and in one word, every thing that hath nought of the City in it may be treated of in *Pastorals*; and that the discourse of Fishers, Plow-men,

Reapers, Hunters, and the like, belong to this kind of Poetry: which according to the Rule that I have laid down cannot be true for, as I before hinted nothing but the action of a 28 Shepherd can be the Subject of a Pastoral.

I shall not here enquire, tho it may seem proper, whether we can decently bring into an Eclogue Reapers, Vine-dressers, Gardners, Fowlers, Hunters, Fishers, or the like, whose lives for the most part are taken up with too much business and employment to have any vacant time for Songs, and idle Chat, which are more agreeable to the leisure of a Sheapards Life: for in a great many Rustick affairs, either the hardship and painful Labor will not admit a song, as in Plowing, or the solitude as in hunting, Fishing, Fowling, and the like; but of this I shall discourse more largely in another place.

Now 'tis not sufficient to make a Poem a true *Pastoral*, that the Subject of it is the action of a Shepherd, for in *Hesiods*erga and *Virgils Georgicks* there are a great many things that belong to the employment of a Shepherd, yet none fancy they are Pastorals; from whence 'tis evident, that beside the *matter*, which we have defin'd to be the action of a Sheapard, there is a peculiar *Form* proper to this kind of *Poetry* by which 'tis distinguish'd from all others.

Of Poetry in General *Socrates*, as *Plato* tells us, would have *Fable* to be the *Form: Aristotle* Imitation: I shall not dispute what difference there is between these two, but only inquire whether Imitation be the *Form* of *Pastoral*: 'Tis certain that *Epick* Poetry is differenc't from *Tragick* on29ly by the manner of imitation, for the latter imitates by *action*, and the former by bare *narration*: But *Pastoral* is the imitation of a *Pastoral* action either by bare narration, as in *Virgil's Alexis*, and *Theocritus's 7th Idyllium,* in which the Poet speaks all along in his own Person: or by action as in *Virgil's Tityrus*, and the first of *Theocritus*, or by both mixt, as in the Second and Eleventh *Idylliums*, in which the Poet partly speaks in his own Person, and partly makes others speak, and I think the old *Scholiast* on *Theocritus* took an hint from these when he says, that Pastoral is a mixture made up of all sorts, for 'tis Narrative, Dramatick, and mixt, and *Aristotle*, tho obscurely, seems to hint in those words, *In every one of the mentioned Arts there is Imitation, in some simple, in some mixt*; now this latter being peculiar to *Bucolicks* makes its very form and Essence: and therefore *Scaliger*, in the 4*th* Chapter of his first Book of Poetry, reckons up three Species of *Pastorals*, the first hath but one Person, the second several, which sing alternately; the third is mixt of both the other: And the same observation is made by *Heinsius* in his Notes on *Theocritus*, for thus he very plainly to our purpose, *the Character of* Bucolicks *is a mixture of all sorts of Characters, Dramatick, Narrative, or mixt*: from all which 'tis very manifest that the manner of *Imitation* which is proper to *Pastorals* is the mixt: for in other kinds of Poetry 'tis one and simple, at least 30 not so manifold; as in *Tragedy Action*: in *Epick* Poetry *Narration*.

Now I shall explain what sort of *Fable*; *Manners, Thought, Expression*, which four are necessary to constitute every kind of Poetry, are proper to this sort.

Concerning the Fable which Aristotle *calls,*synthesin tôn pragmatôn,

I have but one thing to say: this, as the Philosopher hints, as of all other sorts of Poetry, so of Pastoral is the very Soul. and therfore *Socrates* in *Plato* says, that in those Verses which he had made there was nothing wanting but the *Fable*: therefore Pastorals as other kinds of Poetry must have their Fable, if they will be Poetry: Thus in *Virgil's Silenus* which contains the Stories of allmost the whole Fabulous Age, two Shepherds whom *Silenus* had often promis'd a Song, and as often deceived, seize upon him being drunk and asleep, and bind him with wreath'd Flowers; *Ægle* comes in and incourages the timorous youths, and stains his jolly red Face with Blackberries, *Silenus* laughs at their innocent contrivance, and desires to be unbound, and then with a premeditated Song satisfies the Nymph's and Boys Curiosity; The incomparable Poet sings wonders, the Rocks rejoyce, the Vales eccho, and happy *Eurotas* as if *Phoebus* himself sang, hears all, and bids the Laurels that grow upon his Banks listen to, and learn the Song.

31
Happy Eurotas *as he flow'd along*
Heard all, and bad the Laurels learn the Song.

Thus every Eclogue or Idyllium must have its Fable, which must be the groundwork of the whole design, but it must not be perplext with sudden and unlookt for changes, as in *Marinus*'s *Adonis*: for that, tho the *Fable* be of a Shepherd, yet by reason of the strange Bombast under Plots, and wonderful occurences, cannot be accounted *Pastoral*; for that it might be agreeable to the Person it treats of, it must be plain and simple, such as *Sophocles*'s *Ajax*, in which there is not so much as one change of Fortune. As for the Manners, let that precept, which *Horace* lays down in his Epistle to the *Pisones*, be principally observed.

Let each be grac't with that which suits him best.

For this, as 'tis a rule relateing to *Poetry* in general, so it respects this kind also of which we are treating; and against this *Tasso* in his *Amyntas*, *Bonarellus* in his *Phyllis*, *Guarinus* in his *Pastor Fido*, *Marinus* in his *Idylliums*, and most of the *Italians* grievously offend, for they make their *Shepherds* too polite, and elegant, and cloth them with all the neatness of the Town, and Complement of the Court, which tho it may seem very pretty, yet amongst good *Critics*, let *Veratus*32 say what he will in their excuse, it cannot be allowed: For 'tis against *Minturnus*'s Opinion, who in his second Book *de Poetâ* says thus: *Mean Persons are brought in, those in Comedy indeed more polite, those in Pastorals more unelegant, as suppos'd to lead a rude life in Solitude*; and *Jason Denor* a Doctor of *Padua* takes notice of the same as a very absurd Error: *Aristotle* heretofore for a like fault reprehended the *Megarensians*, who observ'd no *Decorum* in their *Theater*, but brought in mean persons with a Train fit for a *King* and cloath'd a Cobler or Tinker in a Purple Robe: In vain doth *Veratus* in his Dispute against *Jason Denor*, to defend those elaborately exquisite discourses, and notable sublime sentences of his *Pastor Fido*, bring some lofty *Idylliums* of *Theocritus*, for those are not acknowledged to be Pastoral; *Theocritus* and *Virgil* must be consulted in this matter, the former designdly makes his Shepherds discourse in the *Dorick* i. e. the Rustick Dialect, sometimes scarce true Grammar; & the other studiously affects ignorance in the persons of his Shepherds, as *Servius* hath observ'd, and is evident in *Melibæus*, who makes *Oaxes* to be a River in *Crete* when 'tis in *Mesopotamia*: and both of them take this way that the Manners may the more exactly suit with the Persons they represent, who of themselves are rude and unpolisht: And this proves that they scandalously err, who make their Shepherds appear polite and elegant; nor can I imagine what *Veratus*33 who makes so much ado about the polite manners of the *Arcadian* Shepherds, would say to *Polybius* who tells us that *Arcadians* by reason of the Mountainousness of the Country and hardness of the weather, are very unsociable and austere.

Now as too much neatness in *Pastoral* is not to be allow'd, so rusticity (I do not mean that which *Plato*, in his Third Book of a Commonwealth, mentions which is but a part of a down right honesty) but Clownish stupidity, such as *Theophrastus*, in his Character of a *Rustick*, describes; or that disagreeable unfashionable roughness which *Horace* mentions in his Epistle to *Lollius*, must not in my opinion be endur'd: On this side *Mantuan* errs extreamly, and is intolerably absur'd, who makes Shepherds blockishly sottish, and insufferably rude: And a certain Interpreter blames *Theocritus* for the same thing, who in some mens opinion sometimes keeps too close to the *Clown*, and is rustick and uncouth; But this may be very well excus'd because the Age in which he sang was not as polite as now.

But that every Part may be suitable to a Shepherd, we must consult unstain'd, uncorrupted Nature; so that the manners might not be too Clownish nor too Caurtly: And this mean may be easily observed if the manners of our Shepherds be represented according to the *Genius* of the *golden Age*, in which, if *Guarinus* may be be34liev'd, every man follow'd that employment: And *Nannius* in the Preface to his Comments on *Virgil's Bucolicks* is of the same opinion, for he requires that the manners might represent the Golden Age: and this was the reason that *Virgil* himself in his *Pollio* describes that Age, which he knew very well was proper to *Bucolicks*: For in the whole course of a Shepherds life there can be no form more excellent than that which was the practise of the Golden Age; And this may serve to moderate and temper the affections that must be exprest in this sort of Poetry, and sufficiently declare the whole Essence of it, which in short must be taken from the nature of a Shepherds life to which a Courtly dress is not agreeable.

That the Thought may be commendable, it must be suitable to the *manners*; as those must be plain and pure that must be so too: nor must contain any, deep, exquisite, or elaborate fancies: And against this the *Italians* offend, who continually hunt after smart witty sayings, very foolishly in my opinion; for in the Country, where all things should be full of plaisness and simplicity who would paint or endeavor to be gawdy when such appearances would be very disagreeable and offend? *Pontanus* in this matter hath said very well, *The Thought must not be to exquisite and witty, the Comparisons obvious and common, such as the State of Persons and Things require*: Yet tho too scrupulous a Curiosity in Ornament ought to be re35jected, yet lest the Thought be cold and flat, it must have some quickness of Passion, as in these.

Cruel Alexis *can't my Verses move?*
Hast thou no Pitty? I must dye for Love.

And again,

He neither Gods, nor yet my Verse regards.

The Sense must not be long, copious, and continued, For*Pastoral* is weak, and not able to hold out; but of this more when I come to lay down rules for its Composure: But tho it ought to imitate *Comedy* in its common way of discourse, yet it must not chose *old Comedy* for its pattern, for that is too impudent, and licentiously abusive: Let it be free and modest, honest and ingenuous, and that will make it agreeable to the Golden Age.

Let the Expression be plain and easy, but elegant and neat, and the purest which the language will afford; *Pontanus* upon *Virgils* Bucolicks gives the very same rule, *In Bucolicks the Expression must be humble, nearer common discourse than otherwise, not very Spirituous and vivid, yet such as shows life and strength*: Tis certain that *Virgil* in his *Bucolicks* useth the same words which *Tully* did in the *Forum* or the *Senate*; and *Tityrus* beneath his shady Beech speaks as pure and good *Latin* as *Augustus* in his Palace, as *Modicius* in his *Apology* for *Virgil* hath excellently observ'd: 36 This rule, 'tis true; *Theocritus* hath not so strictly follow'd, whose Rustick and Pastoral Muse, as *Quintilian* phraseth it, *not only is affraid to appear in the* Forum, *but the City*, and for the very same thing an *Alexandrian* flouts the *Syracucusian Weomen* in the Fifteenth *Idyllium* of *Theocritus*, for when they, being then in the City, spoke the *Dorick* Dialect, the delicate Citizen could not endure it, and found fault with their distastful, as he thought, pronunciation: and his reflection was very smart.

Like Pidgeons you have mouths from Ear to Ear.

So intolerable did that broad way of pronunciation, tho exactly fit for a Clowns discourse, seem to a Citizen: and hence *Probus* observes that 'twas much harder for the *Latines* to write *Pastorals* than for the *Greeks*; because the *Latines* had not some *Dialects* peculiar to the Country, and others to the City, as the *Greeks* had; Besides the *Latine* Language, as *Quintilian* hath observ'd, is not capable of the neatness which is necessary to Bucolicks, no, that is the peculiar priviledge of the *Greeks*: *We cannot*, says he, *be so low, they exceed us in subtlety, and in propriety they are at more certainty than We*: and again, *in pat and close Expressions we cannot reach the Greeks*: And, if we believe *Tully, Greek is much more fit for Ornament than Latin* for it hath much more of that neatness, 37 and ravishing delightfulness, which *Bucolicks* necessarily require.

Yet of Pastoral, with whose Nature we are not very well acquainted, what that *Form* is which the *Greeks* call the *Character*, is not very easy to determine; yet that we may come to some certainty, we must stick to our former observation, *viz.* that *Pastoral* belongs properly to the *Golden Age*: For as *Tully* in his Treatise *de Oratore* says, *in all our disputes the Subject is to be measur'd by the most perfect of that kind*, and *Synesius* in his *Encomium* on *Baldness* hints the very same, when he tells us that Poetry fashions its subject as Men imagine it should be, and not as really it is: pros doxan, ou pros alêtheian: Now the Life of a Shepherd, that it might be rais'd to the highest perfection, is to be referr'd to the manners and age of the world whilst yet innocent, and such as the Fables have describ'd it: And as Simplicity was the principal vertue of that Age, so it ought to be the peculiar Grace, and as it were *Character* of *Bucolicks*: in which the Fable, Manners, Thought, and Expression ought to be full of the most innocent simplicity imaginable: for as Innocence in Life, so purity and simplicity in discourse was the Glory of that Age: So as gravity to *Epicks*, Sweetness to *Lyricks*, Humor to *Comedy*, softness to *Elegies* and smartness to *Epigrams*, so simplicity to *Pastorals* is proper; and one upon *Theocritus* says, *that the Idea of his Bucolicks is in every part pure, and in all 38 that belongs to simplicity very happy*: Such is this of *Virgil, unwholsome to us Singers is the shade*

Of Juniper, 'tis an unwholsome shade:

Than which in my opinion nothing can be more simply; nothing more rustically said; and this is the reason I suppose why *Macrobius* says that this kind of Poetry is creeping and upon mean subjects; and why too *Virgils Tityrus* lying under his shady Beech displeaseth some; Excellent Criticks indeed, whom I wish a little more sense, that they might not really be, what they would not seem to be, *Ridiculous*: *Theocritus* excells *Virgil* in this, of whom *Modicius* says, *Theocritus deserves the greatest commendation for his happy imitation of the simplicity of his Shepherds*, Virgil *hath mixt Allegories, and some other things which contain too much learning, and deepness of Thought for Persons of so mean a Quality*: Yet here I must obviate their mistake who fancy that this sort of *Poetry*, because in it self low and simple, is the proper work of *mean* Wits, and not the most *sublime* and *excellent* perfections: For as I think there be can nothing more elegant than easy naked simplicity, so likewise nothing can require more strength of Wit, and greater pains; and he must be of a great and clear judgment, who attempts *Pastoral*, and comes of with Honor. For there is no part of *Poetry* that requires more spirit, for if any part is not close and well compacted the whole Fabrick will be ruin'd, and the 39 matter, in it self humble, must creep; unless it is held up by the strength and vigor of the *Expression*.

Another qualification and excellence of *Pastoral* is to imitate *Timanthes*'s Art, of whom *Pliny* writes thus; *Timanthes was very Ingenious, in all his peices more was to be understood than the Colours express'd, and tho his Art was very extraordinary yet his Fancy exceeded it*: In this *Virgil* is peculiarly happy, but others, especially raw unexperienced Writers, if they are to describe a Rainbow, or a River, pour out their whole stock, and are unable to contain: Now 'tis properly requisite to a Pastoral that there should be a great deal coucht in a few words, and every thing it says should be so short, and so close, as if its chiefest excellence was to be spareing in Expression: such is that of *Virgil*;

These Fields and Corn shall a Barbarian share?
See the Effects of all our Civil War.

How short is that? how concise? and yet how full of sense in the same *Eclogue*.

I wonder'd why all thy complaints were made,
Absent was Tityrus:

And the like you may every where meet with, as

Mopsus *weds* Nisa, *what may'nt Lovers hope?*

and in the second *Eclogue,*

40
Whom dost thou fly ah frantick! oft the Woods
Hold Gods, and Paris *equal to the Gods.*

This Grace *Virgil* learn'd from *Theocritus,* allmost most all whose Periods; especially in the third *Idyllium,* have no conjunction to connect them, that the sense might be more close, and the Affection vehement and strong: as in this

Let all things change, let Pears the Firs adorn
Now Daphnis *dyes.*

And in the third *Eclogue.*

But when she saw, how great was the surprize! &c.

And any one may find a great many of the like in *Theocritus* and *Virgil,* if with a leisurely delight he nicely examines their delicate Composures: And this I account the greatest grace in *Pastorals,* which in my opinion those that write *Pastorals* do not sufficiently observe: 'Tis true Ours (the *French*) and the *Italian* language is to babling to endure it; This is the Rock on which those that write *Pastorals* in their *Mother* tongue are usually split, But the *Italians* are inevitably lost; who having store of *Wit,* a very subtle invention and flowing fancy, cannot contain; everything that comes into their mind must be poured out, nor are they able to endure the least restraint: as is evident from *Marinus's Idylliums,* and a great many of that nation who have ventur'd on such composures; For unless there are many 41 stops and breakings off in the series of a *Pastoral,* it can neither be pleasing nor artificial: And in my Opinion *Virgil* excells *Theocritus* in this, for *Virgil* is neither so continued, nor so long as *Theocritus;* who indulges too much the garrulity of his *Greek;* nay even in those things which he expresseth he is more close, and more cautiously conceals that part which ought to be dissembled: And this I am sure is a most admirable part of Eloquence; as *Tully* in his Epistle to *Atticus* says, *'Tis rare to speak Eloquently, but more rare to be eloquently silent*: And this unskillful *Criticks* are not acquainted with, and therefore are wont oftner to find fault with that which is not fitly exprest, than commend that which is prudently conceal'd: I could heap up a great many more things to this purpose, but I see no need of such a trouble, since no man can rationally doubt of the goodness of my Observation. Therefore, in short, let him that writes Pastorals think brevity, if it doth not obscure his sense, to be the greatest grace which he can attain.

Now why *Bucolicks* should require such Brevity, and be so essentially sparing in *Expression*, I see no other reason but this: It loves *Simplicity* so much that it must be averse to that Pomp and Ostentation which *Epick* Poetry must show, for that must be copious and flowing, in every part smooth, and equal to it self: But *Pastoral* must dissemble, and hide even that which it would 42 show, like *Damon's Galatea*, who flies then when she most desires to be discovered.

And to the Bushes flys, yet would be seen.

And this doth not proceed from any malitious ill-natur'd Coyness, as some imagine, but from an ingenuous modesty and bashfulness, which usually accompanies, and is a proof of *Simplicity: Tis very rare*, says Pliny, *to find a man so exquisitely skillful, as to be able to show those Features in a Picture which he hides*, and I think it to be so difficult a task, that none but the most excellent Wits can attempt it with success: For small Wits usually abound with a multitude of words.

The third Grace of *Bucolicks* is *Neatness*, which contains all the taking prettiness and sweetness of Expression, and whatsoever is call'd the Delicacies of the more delightful and pleasing *Muses*: This the Rural *Muses* bestow'd on *Virgil*, as *Horace* in the tenth *Satyr* of his first Book says,

And Virgils *happy Muse in Eclogues plays,*
soft and facetious;

Which *Fabius* takes to signify the most taking neatness and most exquisite Elegance imaginable: For thus he explains this place, in which he agrees with *Tully*, who in his *Third Book de Oratore*, says, the *Atticks* are Facetious *i.e.* elegant: Tho the common Interpreters of these words are not of the same mind: But if by *Facetious Horace* had meant *jesting*, and such as is design'd to make men laugh, and apply'd that to *Virgil*, nothing 43 could have been more ridiculous; 'tis the design of *Comedy* to raise laughter, but *Eclogue* should only delight, and charm by its takeing *prettiness*: All ravishing *Delicacies* of Thought, all sweetness of Expression, all that Salt from which *Venus*, as the Poets Fable, rose; are so essential to this kind of *Poetry*, that it cannot endure any thing that is scurillous, malitiously biteing, or ridiculous: There must be nothing in it but *Hony, Milk, Roses, Violets*, and the like sweetness, so that when you read you might think that you are in *Adonis*'s Gardens, as the *Greeks* speak, *i.e.* in the most pleasant place imaginable: For since the subject of *Eclogue* must be mean and unsurprizing, unless it maintains purity and neatness of Expression, it cannot please.

Therefore it must do as *Tully* says his friend *Atticus* did, who entertaining his acquaintance with Leeks and Onions, pleas'd them all very well, because he had them serv'd up in wicker Chargers, and clean Baskets; So let an *Eclogue* serve up its fruits and flowers with some, tho no costly imbellishment, such as may answer to the wicker Chargers, and Baskets; which may be provided at a cheap rate, and are agreeable to the Country: yet, (and this rule if you aim at exact simplicity, can never be too nicely observ'd,) you must most carefully avoid all paint and gawdiness of Expression, and, (which of all sorts of Elegancies is the most difficult to be avoided) 44 you must take the greatest care that no scrupulous trimness, or artificial fineness appear: For, as *Quintilian* teaches, *in some cases diligence and care most most troublesomly perverse*; and when things are most sweet they are next to loathsome and many times degenerate: Therefore as in Weomen a careless dress becomes some extreamly. Thus *Pastoral*, that it might not be uncomely, ought sometimes to be negligent, or the finess of its ornaments ought not to appear and lye open to every bodies view: so that it ought to affect a studied carelessness, and design'd negligence: And that this may be, all gawdiness of Dress, such as Paint and Curls, all artificial shining is to be despis'd, but in the mean time care must be taken that the Expression be bright and simply clean, not filthy and disgustful, but such as is varnisht with Wit and Fancy: Now to perfect this, *Nature* is chiefly to be lookt upon, (for nothing that is disagreeable to Nature can please) yet that will hardly prevail naked, by it self, and without the polishing of Art.

Then there are three things in which, as in its parts, the whole *Character* of a *Pastoral* is contain'd: *Simplicity* of Thought and expression: *Shortness* of Periods full of sense and spirit: and the *Delicacy* of a most elegant ravishing unaffected neatness.

Next I will enquire in to the *Efficient*, and then into the *Final* Cause of *Pastorals*.

45*Aristotle* assigns two efficient Causes of *Poetry*, The natural desire of Imitation in Man whom he calls the most imitative Creature; and Pleasure consequent to that Imitation: Which indeed are the *Remote* Causes, but the *Immediate* are *Art* and *Nature*; Now according to the differences of *Genius*'s several *Species* of Poetry have been introduced. For as the *Philosopher* hath observ'd, diespathê kata ta oikeia êthê hê poiêsis Thus those that were lofty imitated great and Illustrious; those that were low spirited and groveling mean Actions: And every one, according to the various inclination of his *Nature*, follow'd this or that sort of *Poetry*: This the *Philosopher* expresly affirms, And *Dio Chrysostomus* says of *Homer* that he received from the Gods a Nature fit for all sorts of Verse: but this is an happiness which none partake but, as he in the same place intimates, Godlike minds.

Not to mention other kinds of *Poetry*, what particular Genius is requir'd to *Pastoral* I think, is evident from the foregoing Discourse, for as every part of it ought to be full of simple and inartificial neatness, so it requires a Wit naturally neat and pleasant, born to delight and ravish, which are the qualifications certainly of a great and most excellent Nature. For whatsoever in any kind is delicate and elegant, that is usually most excellent: And such a *Genius* that hath a sprightfulness of Nature, and is well instructed 46 by the rules of Art, is fit to attempt *Pastorals*.

Of the end of Pastorals tis not so easy to give an account: For as to the end of Poetry in General: The Enemies of Poets run out into a large common place, and loudly tell us that Poetry is frivolous and unprofitable. Excellent men! that love *profit* perchance, but have no regard for *Honesty* and *Goodness*; who do not know that all excellent *Arts* sprang from *Poetry* at first.

Which what is honest, base, or just, or good,
Better than Crantor, *or* Chrysippus *show'd.*

For tis *Poetry* that like a chast unspotted Virgin, shews men the way, and the means to live happily, who afterward are deprav'd by the immodest precepts of vitiated and impudent *Philosophy.* For every body knows, that the *Epick* sets before us the highest example of the Bravest man; the *Tragedian* regulates the Affections of the Mind; the *Lyrick* reforms Manners, or sings the Praises of Gods, and Heroes; so that there's no part of *Poetry* but hath it's proper end, and profits.

But grant all this true, *Pastoral* can make no such pretence: if you sing a *Hero,* you excite mens minds to imitate his Actions, and notable Exploits; but how can *Bucolicks* apply these or the like advantages to its self? *He that reads 47 Heroick Poems, learns what is the vertue of a Hero, and wishes to be like him; but he that reads Pastorals, neither learns how to feed sheep, nor wishes himself a shepherd:* And a great deal more to this purpose you may see in *Modicius,* as *Pontanus* cites him in his Notes on *Virgil's Eclogues.*

But when tis the end of *Comedy,* as *Jerom* in his Epistle to *Furia* says, to know the Humors of Men, and to describe them; and *Demea* in *Terence* intimates the same thing,

To look on all mens lives as in a Glass,
And take from those Examples for our Own,

so that our Humors and Conversations may be better'd, and improv'd; why may not *Pastoral* be allow'd the same Priviledge, and be admitted to regulate and improve a *Shepherd*'s life by its *Bucolicks*? For since tis a product of the Golden Age, it will shew the most innocent manners of the most ancient Simplicity, how plain and honest, and how free from all varnish, and deceit, to more degenerate, and worse times: And certainly for this tis commendable in its kind, since its design in drawing the image of a Country and Shepherd's life, is to teach Honesty, Candor, and Simplicity, which are the vertues of *private* men; as *Epicks* teach the highest Fortitude, and Prudence, and Conduct, which are the vertues of *Generals,* and *Kings.* And tis ne48cessary to Government, that as there is one kind of *Poetry* to instruct the *Citizens,* there should be another to fashion the manners of the *Rusticks*: which if *Pastoral,* as it does, did not do, yet would it not be altogether frivolous, and idle, since by its taking prettinesses it can delight, and please. It can scarce be imagin'd, how much the most flourishing times of the *Roman* Commonwealth, in which *Virgil* wrote, grew better and brisker by the use of *Pastoral*: with it were *Augustus, Mecænas, Asinius Pollio, Alphenus Varus, Cornelius Gallus*, the most admired Wits of that happy Age, wonderfully pleas'd; for whatever is sweet, and ravishing, is contain'd in this sweetest kind of Poetry. But if we must slight every thing, from which no *profit* is to be hop'd, all pleasures of the Eye and Ear are presently to be laid aside; and those excellent Arts, *Musick*, and *Painting*, with which the best men use to be delighted, are presently to be left off. Nor is it indeed credible, that so many excellent Wits, as have devoted themselves to Poetry, would ever have medled with it, if it had been so empty, idle, and frivolous, as some ridiculously morose imagine; who forsooth are better pleas'd with the severity of *Philosophy*, and her harsh, deform'd impropriety of Expressions. But the judgments of such men are the most contemptible in the world; for when by *Poetry* mens minds are fashioned to generous 49 Humors, Kindness, and the like: those must needs be strangers to all those good qualites, who hate, or proclaim *Poetry* to be frivolous, and useless.

50

The Third PART.

Rules for writing Pastorals.

IN delivering Rules for writing *Pastorals*, I shall not point to the *streams*, which to look after argues a small creeping *Genius*, but lead you to the *fountains*. But first I must tell you, how difficult it is to write *Pastorals*, which many seem not sufficiently to understand: For since its matter is low, and humble, it seems to have nothing that is troublesome, and difficult. But this is a great mistake, for, as *Horace* says of *Comedy*, "It is by so much the more difficult, by how much the less pardonable are the mistakes committed in its composure": and the same is to be thought of every thing, whose end is to please, and delight. For whatsoever is contriv'd for pleasure, and not necessarily requir'd, unless it be exquisite, must be nauseous, and distastful; as at a Supper, scraping Musick, thick Oyntment, or the like, because the Entertainment might have been without all these; For the sweetest things, and most delicious, are most apt to satiate; for tho the sense may sometimes be pleas'd, yet it presently disgusts that which is 51 luscious, and, as *Lucretius* phraseth it,

E'en in the midst and fury of the Joys,
Some thing that's better riseth, and destroys.

Beside, since *Pastoral* is of that nature, that it cannot endure too much negligence, nor too scrupulous diligence, it must be very difficult to be compos'd, especially since the expression must be neat, but not too exquisite, and fine: It must have a simple native beauty, but not too mean; it must have all sorts of delicacies, and surprizing fancies, yet not be flowing, and luxuriant. And certainly, to hit all these excellencies is difficult enough, since Wit, whose nature it is to pour it self forth, must rather be restrain'd than indulg'd; and that force of the Mind, which of it self is so ready to run on, must be checkt, and bridled: Which cannot be easily perform'd by any, but those who have a very good Judgment, and practically skill'd in Arts, and Sciences: And lastly, a neat, and as it were a happy Wit; not that curious sort, I mean, which *Petronius* allows *Horace*, lest too much *Art* should take off the Beauty of the *Simplicity*. And therefore I would not have any one undertake this task, that is not very polite by *Nature*, and very much at leisure. For what is more hard than to be always in the *Country*, and yet never to be *Clownish*? to sing of *mean*, and *trivial* mat52ters, yet not *trivially*, and *meanly*? to pipe on a *slender* Reed, and yet keep the sound from being *harsh*, and *squeaking*? to make every thing *sweet*, yet never *satiate*? And this I thought necessary to premise, in order to the better laying down of such Rules as I design. For the naked *simplicity* both of the Matter and Expression of a *Pastoral*, upon bare Contemplation, might seem easily to be hit, but upon trial 'twill be found a very hard task: Nor was the difficulty to be dissembled, lest *Ignorance* should betray some into a rash attempt. Now I must come to the very Rules; for as nothing excellent can be brought to perfection without *Nature*, (for Art unassisted by that, is vain, and ineffectual,) so there is no *Nature* so excellent, and happy, which by its own strength, and without *Art* and *Use* can make any thing excellent, and great.

But tis hard to give *Rules* for that, for which there have been none already given; for where there are no footsteps nor path to direct, I cannot tell how any one can be certain of his way. Yet in this difficulty I will follow *Aristotle*'s Example, who being to lay down Rules concerning *Epicks*, propos'd *Homer* as a Pattern, from whom he deduc'd the whole Art: So I will gather from *Theocritus* and *Virgil*, those Fathers of *Pastoral*, what I shall deliver on this account. For all the Rules that are to be given of any Art, are to be given of it as excellent, and perfect, and 53 therefore ought to be taken from them in whom it is so.

The first Rule shall be about the *Matter*, which is either the *Action* of a *Shepherd*, or contriv'd and fitted to the *Genius* of a Shepherd; for tho *Pastoral* is simple, and bashful, yet it will entertain lofty subjects, if it can be permitted to turn and fashion them to its own proper Circumstances, and Humor: which tho *Theocritus* hath never done, but kept close to *pastoral* simplicity, yet *Virgil* hath happily attempted; of whom almost the same *Character* might be given, which *Quintilian* bestow'd on *Stesichorus*, who *with his Harp bore up the most weighty subjects of* Epick *Poetry*; for *Virgil* sang great and lofty things to his Oaten Reed, but yet suited to the Humor of a Shepherd, for every thing that is not agreeable to that, cannot belong to *Pastoral*: of its own nature it cannot treat of lofty and great matters.

Therefore let *Pastoral* be smooth and soft, not noisy and bombast; lest whilst it raiseth its voice, and opens its mouth, it meet with the same fate that, they say, an *Italian* Shepherd did, who having a very large mouth, and a very strong breath, brake his Pipe as often as he blow'd it. This is a great fault in one that writes *Pastorals*: for if his words are too sounding, or his sense too strong, he must be absurd, because indecently loud. And this is not the rule of an unskilful 54 impertinent Adviser, but rather of a very excellent Master in this *Art*; for *Phoebus* twitcht *Virgil* by the Ear, and warn'd him to forbear great Subjects: but if it ventures upon such, it may be allow'd to use some short *Invocations*, and, as *Epicks* do, modestly implore the assistance of a Muse. This *Virgil* doth in his *Pollio*, which is a Composure of an unusual loftiness:

Sicilian *Muse begin a loftier strain.*

So he invocates *Arethusa*, when *Cornelius Gallus Proconsul of Ægypt* and his *Amours*, matters above the common reach of *Pastoral*, are his Subject.

One Labor more O Arethusa *yield.*

Why he makes his application to *Aretheusa* is easy to conjecture, for she was a *Nymph* of *Sicily*, and so he might hope that she could inspire him with a *Genius* fit for *Pastorals* which first began in that *Island*, Thus in the seventh and eighth *Eclogue*, as the matter would bear, he invocates the Nymphs and Muses: And *Theocritus* does the same,

Tell Goddess, you can tell.

From whence 'tis evident that in *Pastoral*, tho it never pretends to any greatness, *Invocations*55 may be allow'd: But whatever Subject it chooseth, it must take care to accommodate it to the Genius and Circumstances of a Shepherd. Concerning the Form, or mode of *Imitation*, I shall not repeat what I have already said, *viz.* that this is in it self *mixt*; for *Pastoral* is either *Alternate*, or hath but *one Person*, or is *mixt* of both: yet 'tis properly and chiefly *Alternate.* as is evident from that of *Theocritus.*

Sing Rural *strains, for as we march along*
We may delight each other with a Song.

In which the *Poet* shows that *alternate* singing is proper to a *Pastoral*: But as for the *Fable*, 'tis requisite that it should be simple, lest in stead of *Pastoral* it put on the form of a *Comedy*, or *Tragedy* if the *Fable* be great, or intricate: It must be *One*; this *Aristotle* thinks necessary in every *Poem*, and *Horace* lays down this general Rule,

Be every Fable *simple, and but one*:

For every Poem, that is not *One*, is imperfect, and this *Unity* is to be taken from the *Action*: for if that is *One*, the Poem will be so too. Such is the Passion of *Corydon* in *Virgil*'s second Eclogue, *Meliboeus*'s Expostulation with *Tityrus* about his Fortune; *Theocritus*'s *Thyrsis*, *Cyclops*, and *Amaryllis*, of which perhaps in its proper place I may treat more largely. 56 Let the third Rule be concerning the *Expression*, which cannot be in this kind excellent unless borrow'd from

Theocritus's *Idylliums*, or *Virgil*'s *Eclogues*, let it be chiefly simple, and ingenuous: such is that of *Theocritus*,

A Kid belongs to thee, and Kids are good,

    Or that in *Virgil*'s seventh Eclogue,

This Pail of Milk, these Cakes (Priapus) *every year*
Expect; a little Garden is thy care:
Thou'rt Marble now, but if more Land I hold,
If my Flock thrive, thou shalt be made of Gold,

    than which I cannot imagine more simple, and more ingenuous expressions. To which may be added that out of his *Palemon*,

And I love Phyllis, *for her Charms excell;*
At my departure O what tears there fell!
She sigh'd, Farewell Dear Youth, a long Farewell.

    Now, That I call an ingenuous Expression which is clear and smooth, that swells with no insolent words, or bold metaphors, but hath something familiar, and as it were obvious in its Composure, and not disguis'd by any study'd and affected dress: All its Ornament must be like the Corn and fruits in the Country, easy to 57 be gotten, and ready at hand, not such as requires Care, Labor, and Cost to be obtain'd: as *Hermogenes* on *Theocritus* observes; *See how easie and unaffected this sounds,*

Pines murmurings, Goatherd, are a pleasing sound,

    and most of his expressions, not to say all, are of the same nature: for the ingenuous simplicity both of Thought and Expression is the natural *Characteristick* of *Pastoral*. In this *Theocritus* and *Virgil* are admirable, and excellent, the others despicable, and to be pittied; for they being enfeebled by the meanes of their subject, either creep, or fall flat. *Virgil* keeps himself up by his choice and curious words, and tho his matter for the most part (and *Pastoral* requires it) is mean, yet his expressions never flag, as is evident from these lines in his *Alexis*:

The glossy Plums I'le bring, and juicy Pear,
Such as were once delightful to my Dear:
I'le crop the Laurel, and the Myrtle tree,
Confus'dly set, because their Sweets agree.

For since the matter must be low, to avoid being abject, and despicable, you must borrow some light from the Expression; not such as is dazling, but pure, and lambent, such as may shine thro the whole matter, but never flash, and blind. 58 The words of such a *Stile* we are usually taught in our Nurses armes, but 'tis to be perfected and polished by length of time, frequent use, study, and diligent reading of the most approved Authors: for Pastoral is apt to be slighted for the meaness of its Matter, unless it hath some additional Beauty, be pure, polisht, and so made pleasing, and attractive. Therefore never let any one, that designs to write *Pastorals*, corrupt himself with foreign manners; for if he hath once vitiated the healthful habit, as I may say, of Expression, which *Bucolicks* necessarily require, 'tis impossible he should be fit for that task. Yet let him not affect pompous or dazling Expressions, for such belong to *Epicks*, or *Tragedians*. Let his words sometimes tast of the Country, not that I mean, of which *Volusius*'s Annals, upon which *Catullus* hath made that biting *Epigram*, are full; for though the Thought ought to be rustick, and such as is suitable to a Shepherd, yet it ought not to be Clownish, as is evident in *Corydon*, when he makes mention of his Goats.

Young sportive Creatures, and of spotted hue,
Which suckled twice a day, I keep for you:
These Thestilis *hath beg'd, and beg'd in vain,*
But now they're Hers, since You my Gifts disdain.

For what can be more Rustical, than to design those *Goats* for *Alexis*, at that very time when 59 he believes *Thestylis*'s winning importunity will be able to prevail? yet there is nothing Clownish in the words. In short, *Bucolicks* should deserve that commendation which *Tully* gives *Crassus*, of whose Orations he would say, *that nothing could be more free from childish painting, and affected finery.* So let the Expression in *Pastoral* be without gawdy trappings, and all those little fineries of Art, which are us'd to set off and varnish a discourse: But let an ingenuous Simplicity. and unaffected pleasing Neatness appear in every part; which yet will be flat, if 'tis drawn out to any length, if not close, short, and broken, as that in *Virgil*,

He that loves Bavius *Verses, hates not Thine*:

And in the same *Eclogue*,

--It is not safe to drive too nigh,
The Bank may fail, the Ram is hardly dry:

And in *Corydon*,

To learn this Art what won't Amyntas *do*?

And in *Theocritus* much of the same nature may be seen; as in his other *Pastoral Idylliums*, so chiefly in his fifth. Thus *Battus* in the fourth *Idyllium*, complaining for the loss of *Amaryllis*, 60

Dear Nymph, dear as my Goats, you dy'd.

And how soft and tender is that in the third *Idyllium*,

And she may look on me, she may be won,
She may be kind, she is not perfect Stone,

And in this *concise*, close way of Expression lies the chiefest Grace of *Pastorals*: for in my opinion there's nothing in the whole Composition that can delight more than those frequent stops, and breakings off. Yet lest in these too it become dull and sluggish, it must be quickned by frequent lively touches of Concernment: such as that of the Goatherd in the third Idyllium,

--I see that I must die:

Or *Daphnis*'s despair, which *Thyrsis* sings in the first *Idyllium*,

Ye Wolves, and Pards, and Mountain Bores adieu,
The Herdsmen now must walk no more with You.

How tender are the lines, and yet what passion they contain! And most of *Virgil*'s are of this nature, but there are likewise in him some touches of despairing Love, such as is this of *Alphesiboeus*,

Nor have I any mind to be reliev'd:

61Or that of *Damon*,

I'le dy, yet tell my Love e'en whilst I dy:

Or that of *Corydon*,

He lov'd, but could not hope for Love again.

For tho *Pastoral* doth not admit any violent passions, such as proceed from the greatest extremity, and usually accompany despair; yet because Despairing Love is not attended with those frightful and horrible consequences, but looks more like *grief to be pittied*, and a *pleasing madness*, than *rage* and *fury*, *Eclogue* is so far from refusing, that it rather loves, and passionately requires them. Therefore an unfortunate *Shepherd* may be brought in, complaining of his successless Love to the *Moon, Stars*, or *Rocks*, or to the Woods, and purling Streams, mourning the unsupportable anger, the frowns and coyness of his proud *Phyllis*; singing at his *Nymphs* door, (which *Plutarch* reckons among the signs of Passion) or doing any of those fooleries, which are familiar to Lovers. Yet the Passion must not rise too high, as *Polyphemus's*, *Galateas's* mad Lover, of whom *Theocritus* divinely thus, as almost of every thing else:

His was no common flame, nor could he move
In the old Arts, and beaten paths of Love,
No Flowers nor Fruits sent to oblige the Fair,
His was all Rage, and Madness:
62

For all violent Perturbations are to be diligently avoided by *Bucolicks*, whose nature it is to be *soft*, and *easie*: For in small matters, and such must all the strifes and contentions of Shepherds be, to make a great deal of adoe, is as unseemly, as to put *Hercules's* Vizard and Buskins on an Infant, as *Quintilian* hath excellently observ'd. For since *Eclogue* is but weak, it seems not capable of those Commotions which belong to the *Theater*, and *Pulpit*; they must be soft, and gentle, and all its Passion must seem to flow only, and not break out: as in *Virgil's Gallus*,

Ah, far from home and me You wander o're
The Alpine *snows, the farthest Western shore,*
And frozen Rhine. *When are we like to meet?*
Ah gently, gently, lest thy tender feet
Sharp Ice may wound.

To these he may sometimes joyn some short Interrogations made to *inanimate Beings*, for those spread a strange life and vigor thro the whole Composure. Thus in *Daphnis*,

Did not You Streams, and Hazels, hear the Nymphs?

Or give the very Trees, and Fountains sense, as in *Tityrus*,

Thee (Tityrus) *the Pines, and every Vale,*
The Fountains, Hills, and every shrub did call:

for by this the Concernment is express'd; and of the like nature is that of *Thyrsis*, in *Virgil*'s *Meliboeus*, 63

When Phyllis *comes, my wood will all be green.*

And this sort of Expressions is frequent in *Theocritus*, and *Virgil*, and in these the delicacy of *Pastoral* is principally contain'd, as one of the old *Interpreters* of *Theocritus* hath observ'd on this line, in the eighth *Idyllium*,

Ye Vales, and Streams, a race Divine:

But let them be so, and so seldom us'd, that nothing appear vehement, and bold, for Boldness and Vehemence destroy the sweetness which peculiarly commends *Bucolicks*, and in those Composures a constant care to be soft and easie should be chief: For *Pastoral* bears some resemblance to *Terence*, of whom *Tully*, in that Poem which he writes to *Libo*, gives this Character,

His words are soft, and each expression sweet.

In mixing *Passion* in *Pastorals*, that rule of *Longinus*, in his golden Treatise peri hypsous, must be observ'd, *Never use it, but when the matter requires it, and then too very sparingly.* Concerning the *Numbers*, in which *Pastoral* should be written, this is my opinion; the *Heroick* Measure, but not so strong and sounding as in *Epicks*, is to be chosen. *Virgil* and *Theocritus* have given us examples; for tho *Theocritus* hath in one Idyllium mixt other Numbers, yet that can be of no force against all the rest; and *Virgil* useth no Numbers but *Heroick*, from whence it may be inferr'd, that those are the fittest. 64*Pastoral* may sometimes admit plain, but not long *Narrations* such as *Socrates* in *Plato* requires in a Poet; for he chiefly approves those who use a plain *Narration*, and commends that above all other which is short, and fitly expresseth the nature of the Thing. Some are of opinion that *Bucolicks* cannot endure Narrations, especially if they are very long, and imagine there are none in *Virgil*: but they have not been nice enough in their observations, for there are some, as that in *Silenus*.

Young Chromis *and* Mnasylus *chanct to stray,*
Where (sleeping in a Cave) Silenus *lay,*
Whose constant Cups fly fuming to his brain,
And always boyl in each extended vein:
His trusty Flaggon, full of potent Juice,
Was hanging by, worn out with Age, and Use, &c.

But, because *Narrations* are so seldom to be found in *Theocritus*, and *Virgil*, I think they ought not to be often us'd; yet if the matter will bear it, I believe such as *Socrates* would have, may very fitly be made use of. The Composure will be more suitable to the Genius of a Shepherd, if now and then there are some short turns and digressions from the purpose: Such is that concerning *Pasiphae* in *Silenus*, although tis almost too long; but we may give *Virgil* a little leave, who takes so little liberty himself. 65 Concerning *Descriptions* I cannot tell what to lay down, for in this matter our Guides, *Virgil*, and *Theocritus*, do not very well agree. For he in his first *Idyllium* makes such a long immoderate description of his *Cup*, that *Criticks* find fault with him, but no such description appears in all *Virgil*; for how sparing is he in his description of *Meliboeus*'s Beechen Pot, the work of Divine *Alcimedon*? He doth it in *five* verses, *Theocritus* runs out into *thirty*, which certainly is an argument of a wit that is very much at leisure, and unable to moderate his force. That *shortness* which *Virgil* hath prudently made choice of, is in my opinion much better; for a Shepherd, who is naturally incurious, and unobserving, cannot think that tis his duty to be exact in particulars, and describe every thing with an accurate niceness: yet *Roncardus* hath done it, a man of most correct judgment, and, in imitation of *Theocritus*, hath, considering the then poverty of our language, admirably and largely describ'd *his* Cup; and *Marinus* in his Idylliums hath follow'd the same example. He never keeps within compass in his Descriptions, for which he is deservedly blam'd; let those who would be thought accurate, and men of judgment, follow *Virgil*'s prudent moderation. Nor can the Others gain any advantage from *Moschus*'s *Europa*, in which the description of the *Basket* is very long, for that Idyllium is not *Pastoral*; yet I confess, that some 66 descriptions of such trivial things, if not minutely accurate, may, if seldom us'd, be decently allow'd a place in the discourses of *Shepherds*.

But tho you must be sparing in your *Descriptions*, yet your *Comparisons* must be frequent, and the more often you use them, the better and more graceful will be the Composure; especially if taken from such things, as the Shepherds must be familiarly acquainted with: They are frequent in *Theocritus* but so proper to the Country, that none but a *Shepherd* dare use them. Thus *Menalcas* in the eighth Idyllium:

Rough Storms to Trees, to Birds the treacherous Snare,
Are frightful Evils; Springes to the Hare,
Soft Virgins Love to Man, &c.

And *Damoetas* in *Virgil's Palæmon*,

Woolves sheep destroy, Winds Trees when newly blown,
Storms Corn, and me my Amaryllis *frown.*

And that in the eighth *Eclogue*,

As Clay grows hard, Wax soft in the same fire,
So Daphnis *does in one extream desire.*

And such *Comparisons* are very frequent in him, and very suitable to the Genius of a Shepherd; as likewise often *repetitions*, and doublings of some words: which, if they are luckily plac'd have an unexpressible quaintness, and make the Numbers extream sweet, and the turns ravishing and delightful. An instance of this we have in *Virgil's Meliboeus*,

Phyllis *the Hazel loves; whilst* Phyllis *loves that Tree,*
Myrtles than Hazels of less fame shall be.
67

As for the *Manners* of your *Shepherds*, they must be such as theirs who liv'd in the Islands of the Happy or Golden Age: They must be candid, simple, and ingenuous; lovers of Goodness, and Justice, affable, and kind; strangers to all fraud, contrivance, and deceit; in their Love modest, and chast, not one suspitious word, no loose expression to be allowed: and in this part *Theocritus* is faulty, *Virgil* never; and this difference perhaps is to be ascrib'd to their Ages, the times in which the latter liv'd being more polite, civil, and gentile. And therefore those who make wanton Love- stories the subject of Pastorals, are in my opinion very unadvis'd; for all sort of lewdness or debauchery are directly contrary to the *Innocence* of the *golden*

Age. There is another thing in which *Theocritus* is faulty, and that is making his Shepherds too sharp, and abusive to one another; *Comatas* and *Lacon* are ready to fight, and the railing between those two is as bitter as *Billingsgate*: Now certainly such Raillery cannot be suitable to those sedate times of the Happy Age.

As for *Sentences*, if weighty, and Philosophical, common Sense tells us they are not fit for a *Shepherd's* mouth. Here *Theocritus* cannot be altogether excus'd, but *Virgil* deserves no reprehension. But *Proverbs* justly challenge admission into *Pastorals*, nothing being more common in 68 the mouths of Countrymen than old Sayings.

Thus much seem'd necessary to be premis'd out of *RAPIN*, for the direction and information of the Reader.